To children everywhere who dream of freedom
for themselves and their friends.
—D. B.

To JP, David, Isabel, Guillermo y Gala.
And to Gustavito, our first border-born baby.
Este es pa'ustedes, morritos.
—E. M.

KOKILA
An imprint of Penguin Random House LLC, New York

First published in the United States of America by Kokila, an imprint of Penguin Random House LLC, 2021

Text copyright © 2021 by David Bowles
Illustrations copyright © 2021 by Erika Meza

Kokila & colophon are registered trademarks of Penguin Random House LLC.

Visit us online at penguinrandomhouse.com.

Library of Congress Cataloging-in-Publication Data is available.

Manufactured in China
ISBN 9780593111048

1 3 5 7 9 10 8 6 4 2

Design by Jasmin Rubero
Text set in Lomba Family

The art for this book was created using gouache, watercolor,
pencil and digital gimmicks.

MY TWO BORDER TOWNS

by David Bowles

illustrated by Erika Meza

Kokila

Every other Saturday, my dad wakes me up early.
"Come on, m'ijo," he says. "Vamos al Otro Lado."

The Other Side is not so far away.
Just down the road, right past my school.

Mamá gives us a kiss and a list.
It's different every time we go.

I grab my special bag, hold it tight
as I follow Dad, thinking of what's inside for my friends.

As we drive through town, we pass my favorite spots.
Neighbors line up early for Daisy's yummy pastries.

At a stoplight, Dad calls to the newspaper man,
holding out a dollar. "Aquí tiene, Don Memo. Thanks!"

Before I know it, we reach the broad river,
a watery serpent that glints with the dawn.

Dad reminds me: Coahuiltecans once lived here,
before all this was Mexico—both riverbanks.

Now we're two countries.
We pay to cross.

"Morning," says the U.S. customs guard,
taking Dad's cash with a sleepy frown.

On the other bank, the great eagle greets us.
Dad waves at the soldiers, and they tip their caps.

No one searches through my bag this time.
I say thanks to the Virgen.

We drive up the narrow main street
till Don Chava flags us down and helps us park.

He and my dad shake hands. "Le cuido la troca,"
he says with a smile. "You and your boy have fun."

This town's a twin of the one where I live,
with Spanish spoken everywhere just the same,

but English mostly missing till it pops up
like grains of sugar on a chili pepper.

We have breakfast in our favorite restorán.
Dad sips café de olla while I drink chocolate.

"First up on the list," my dad announces,
"we visit your tíos and pick up Mom's earrings."

Down uneven sidewalks, our feet tap-tap-tap
to trumpet tunes bouncing out of stores.

el auténtico sabor Jaliciense

Arts and Crafts

Shopping Center

Wholesale & Retail

ELOTES   ELOTES

BIRRIA AL HORNO
Don Chinono
DE JALISCO PA TIJUANA

We weave our way through street-side stalls,
chatting with vendors, promising we'll be back.

When we reach my aunt and uncle's jewelry shop,
I give them big hugs and high-five my cousins.

Tío Mateo starts complaining about the town mayor.
My brain gets so bored, I can't stop my yawns!

My primos whisk me away
to play soccer in the vacant lot next door.

It gets hot, so we're lucky the paletero comes by—
we cool our tongues with paletas, mango and melón!

Suddenly, Dad joins in for a dribble and goal,
then he reminds me—we have more to do.

Walking back, we check our list. For ourselves
we need Mexican Cokes, avocados, a jar of honey.

The list says our friends need T-shirts, chanclas, bottled water.
I think they need cold, sweet Gansitos and lots of chewy Glorias, too!

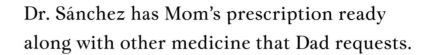

Dr. Sánchez has Mom's prescription ready
along with other medicine that Dad requests.

We load up our truck. Dad gives Don Chava a tip.
Before we head for home, there's one last stop!

The most important visit, Dad says.
We have a duty to care for our gente.

I nod and pick up my bag, full of my favorite comics,
notebooks and pencils, game cartridges.

I add the things we bought today.
I hope all the kids will enjoy them.

As we get on the bridge, Dad pulls to one side:
I jump out with the bag and look for my friend.

A line of people camp along the edge,
entire families from the Caribbean and Central America.

Refugees, Dad calls them.
Stuck between two countries.

The U.S. says there's no room, and Mexico says
it can hardly look after its own gente.

Élder sees me and rushes over. His hair is longer
than when we first met, almost six months back.

"¡Asere!" he shouts. "¡Mi cuate!" I reply.
We do our special handshake and I give him the bag.

Élder's dad joins my dad in the truck. The line crawls on.
I show Élder each item, explaining my choices.

We give his mother the medicine. She tells me a joke,
and the other kids gather to borrow comics.

Dad honks. "Till next time, amigo!" I say,
hugging Élder and heading for the truck.

An hour goes by before we're halfway across.
We take out our passports—

cards that give us the freedom
to travel back and forth.

"I wish Élder could come to our town," I whisper.
"We could jump on my trampoline and draw our own comic."

"Soon, m'ijo," Dad says. "It's unfair to make him wait,
  since our country has room for his family right now.

"But when they get their chance at last,
  we'll welcome them with open arms."

All the way home I imagine a wonderful day,
when all my friends from the Other Side
can go back and forth
between my two
border towns,
just like me.

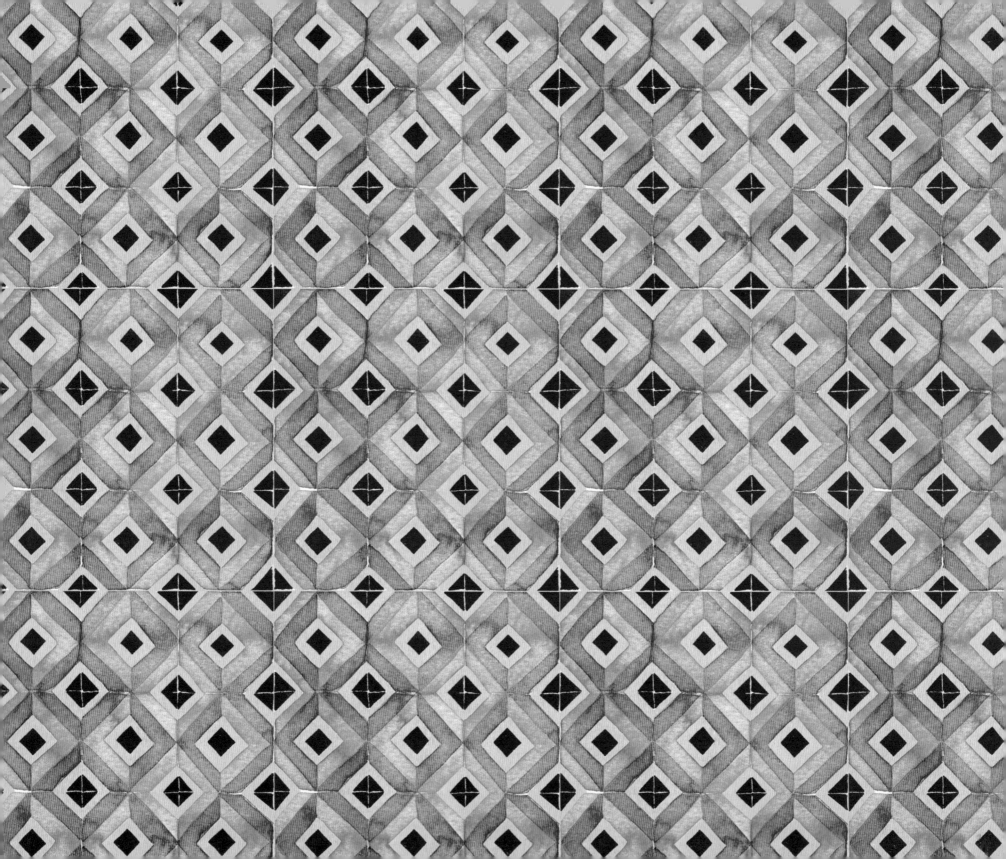